FREDERICK WARNE
An Imprint of Penguin Random House LLC, New York

First published in the United States of America in 2020 by Frederick Warne, an imprint of Penguin Random House LLC, New York.
Manufactured in China

Visit us online at www.penguinrandomhouse.com.

ISBN: 9780241409220

001

PETER RABBIT™

I LOVE YOU, DADDY

in THIS
WORLD
that's
SO WIDE,

IS A
little BIT
EASIER

WHEN
we're
TOGETHER

I love TO EXPLORE,

ROUND *every*
CORNER *and*

through
EVERY
DOOR.

AS the
SUN
sets

AND OUR
playtime
ENDS,

we
WALK *holding*
HANDS,

the
BEST of
FRIENDS.

AND IF
I have
WORRIES

AT the END of THE DAY,

your
KISSES *and*
CUDDLES

chase
THEM
AWAY.

AND as
I DREAM

I KNOW *you will* TRY

TO *make*
them COME
TRUE.

that
YOU
SAY
and
DO,

and
REMEMBER,
DADDY,
I love